TO CESSIE,

I HOPE

EIGHT BELLES,
TRIUMPH BEYOND THE WIRE

MARIA MICHALAK

authorHOUSE®

AuthorHouse™
1663 Liberty Drive, Suite 200
Bloomington, IN 47403
www.authorhouse.com
Phone: 1-800-839-8640

First published by AuthorHouse 3/23/2009

ISBN: 978-1-4389-5808-8 (sc)
ISBN: 978-1-4389-5809-5 (hc)

Printed in the United States of America
Bloomington, Indiana

This book is printed on acid-free paper.

Cover Design by Jack McCartney, Shootin Starz Photography.

DEDICATION

This book is dedicated with much love to the gray filly, Eight Belles.

Thank you for running with all of your heart, sweet girl. You may not have won the blanket of roses, but you won more hearts than there are roses in the blanket! You won't ever be forgotten, sweetheart. You'll be remembered forever, and you will always, always be loved. Thank you for an amazing last race. Enjoy being Home. We miss you! Goodbye for now, heaven's filly.

ACKNOWLEDGEMENTS

My Heavenly Father: All the glory, honor, and praise goes to You! I know I can't do anything without You. Thank You!

Mom and Dad: Thanks for letting me dream big! Dad, thank you for telling me to 'go for it' and for being my 'agent' during some of the publishing process. Mom, thank you for always telling me to 'get going.' Thank you both for your love, for all you do, and for listening to me talk about the biography non-stop for months! This book wouldn't have happened without you! I'm more convinced than ever that I have the best parents out there!

Larry and Cindy Jones: Thank you both so much for all of your help and support. Thank you for letting your faith shine through you! It was an honor for me to write about Eight Belles, and I feel so blessed to have been able to learn more about her as I wrote her story. But her having such awesome trainers made writing and learning about her even more special. Thank you for pouring so much love onto and into that precious gray filly. She really was trained by the best of the best! Thank you so much for everything!

Jen Roytz: You were the first one to help kick this project into motion! Thank you for everything, especially for helping me find information on Eight Belles as a foal and for trying to teach me a little bit about the racing world.

Sandi Danner: Thank you for being so encouraging and such a blessing to me! Thank you so much for believing I could reach the high goals. The project wouldn't have been the same without you there. Thank you for all you did for me, from answering questions about races to being ready to help if I needed you. Thanks, Sandi.

Victoria Keith: Thank you for giving me the 'go ahead' to start writing, for answering my little questions that snowballed into longer questions, for helping me to get more information on Eight Belles, and for always offering what you called your 'two cents.' Thanks for everything!

Rick Porter: Thank you for giving me permission to write Eight Belles' story!

A big thank you to the cover designer and photographers: Jack McCartney, Kat Cerruti, and Candice Chavez. Thank you all so much for your help. You were all great to work with, and you all have such awesome pictures! I loved looking at them over and over again as I was working.

Jack, special thanks to you for an amazing book cover! I was so excited when I found out that you were going to do the book cover for me, and you sure didn't disappoint; you did a great job on it. Thank you so much!

Kat, I have lots to thank you for. Thank you for being such a special sister in Christ and for always being there. Thank you for always listening, for your insight, and for letting the Lord work through you to help give me some peace after Eight Belles went down. Thank you for always giving me pictures that kept me inspired! I, for one, am so glad that you rarely go anywhere without your camera! Thanks for everything.

Candice, thank you, also, for giving me pictures to help keep me inspired. Your pictures are one of a kind and I'm so glad to have them in here. Thank you so much for going into high gear to get last-minute pictures to me and for doing all you could to help me!

Also Thanks To:

Gabriel Saez, Ron Stevens, Jane Dunn, Charity Fillmore, Christina Morgan-Cornett, and Kristen Mueller: Thank you all so, so much for sharing your memories of Eight Belles with me. The book wouldn't be complete without you. Thank you!

Ray and Elizabeth Abbott: Thank you for being there for me all of the time and for helping me whenever I needed you. Thank you for your prayers and your support!

Jason Wells: Your stories and memories of Eight Belles as a yearling were one of the highlights of the 'book journey' for me! Your stories are priceless and I feel blessed to have been able to put them in here. Thank you!

Sharon Whitby: Thank you for being such a great editor! I couldn't have asked for a better one; you were a lot of fun to work with. This book would be full of typos and more without you, that's for sure! Thanks for all you did to help me!

Chris Newsom: Thanks for helping me through some of the 'rocky spots.' Thanks for doing everything from copy and pasting to digging through the internet to find information I needed. You were just a huge help through the whole thing!

Jeff Gaulin: Thank you for taking time to give me legal advice when I needed it.

Ruben Munoz: Without you, I wouldn't have been able to get Gabriel's memories. Thank you so much for your help!

Jack Wortman: Thank you for your stories of Eight Belles, and thank you for your encouraging words!

Frederick Jones: Thank you for sharing your Kentucky Derby, 2008, experience with me. You did a great job of getting me to picture what it was like to be on the backside that day.

Stephanie Jones and Sharon Liles Barnes: Thank you for letting me use your poems! They're beautiful.

Joni Massengale and Bloodhorse.com: Thank you for letting me use comments and signatures from your websites.

Seth Kochera: I have to thank you for sharing both your horse-racing knowledge and 'your' filly, Away's 2007 foal, with me. Away 07 will always be pretty special to me!

Gayle Gorby: Thank you for your support, encouragement, and prayers. You always had a prayer ready and a kind word or two to make me smile! Thank you!

Sharon Poarch: Thank you for helping me to get the manuscript, pictures, and book cover all safely to the publishers!

Katie Boden: Thank you for introducing me to the world of horse-racing! If it hadn't been for you taping the 07 Triple Crown races, I might never have gotten into horse-racing. (Awful thought!) Thanks for always being excited right along with me!

My siblings: Markus, thanks for giving up hours of computer time so I could work. Hannah, thanks for being my fellow horse-racing fan. Martha and Sky, I'm just blessed to have you for 'baby' sisters!

My riding students: My own special little fan club! Thanks for being my own wonderful 'team.' I remember when all of this first began and no one but my family and you knew that I was trying to write the book. Even back then, you all had so much faith that the book was going to happen. Thanks for everything! You guys are awesome.

My 'Herd': Okay, so most writers probably don't put their horses on the thanks page. But my horses are some of my best friends and they're always there for me! Belle, Taffy, and Sundae, thanks for being my precious girls and for listening to me talk about this other girl named 'Eight Belles' all of the time. And to Jones, my newest addition: Thank you for being my sweet boy!

To the others:

To those I missed, thanks so much to you, too! So, so many people have encouraged me, prayed for me, and helped me during the making of this book. Even the simple words "good luck with your book" put a smile on my face and pushed me to keep going. Special thanks to everyone that took care of Eight Belles. I know there were so many that gave her love and cared for her while she was here. Thank you.

Thank you, everyone, from the bottom of my heart! God bless you all!

INTRODUCTION

"She was a magnificent steel gray filly who will live in our hearts forever." - Rick Porter, owner of Fox Hill Farm and Eight Belles

This is a true story about a filly, a special gray filly who touched thousands of hearts during the short time she was on earth.

"Nobody's close to Eight Belles!" -race-caller on October 30, 2007; Maiden Special Weight at Delaware Park, Delaware

It's about a filly who left the others in the dust while breaking her maiden!

"She had incredible heart, mind, and speed." -Gabriel Saez, jockey

"Eight Belles is fleeing the scene!" -race-caller on January 21, 2008; Allowance at Fair Grounds, Louisiana

It's about a filly with all of the heart, grace, and courage it takes to be a champion.

"She just oozed with class in everything she did." -Jason Wells, yearling groom

"And it's a superstar in the making!" -race-caller, March 16, 2008; Honeybee Stakes at Oaklawn Park, Arkansas

It's about a filly who galloped right into the racing world's spotlight and onto a road to the Kentucky Derby.

"She had a big heart. She would do anything you asked her to do." -Charity Fillmore, rider at Holly Hill Training Center

"And it's Eight Belles! A surge at the wire!" -race-caller, April 6, 2008; Fantasy Stakes at Oaklawn Park, Arkansas

It's about a filly who had all it took to run in the "greatest two minutes in horse-racing." It's about a filly ready to run against nineteen colts in the Run for the Roses.

"She went out in glory. She went out a champion to us."
-Larry Jones, Eight Belles' trainer

"The filly Eight Belles is trying to run him down in the final furlong .... EIGHT BELLES was second!" - race-caller, May 3, 2008; Kentucky Derby at Churchill Downs

It's about a filly who finished her race in glory. It's about a filly who galloped out for the last time to the roar of thousands.

It's about a filly who triumphed beyond the wire of her last race. She triumphed by changing the sport of kings, by saving other horses, and by touching thousands of people across the nation, and across the world.

It's the life story of Eight Belles, runner up in the 134th Kentucky Derby.

Picture by Candice Chavez

- 1 -

"She was just a nice baby that everyone liked."
- Three Chimneys Farm

"And Unbridled's Song takes the lead!" the race-caller shouted as a dark gray colt surged forward in the 1995 Breeder's Cup Juvenile. The two-year-old Unbridled's Song battled hard with a colt named Hennessy. Coming down the stretch, it was a two-horse race.

The crowd was on their feet and cheering, loving the stretch duel. Would Hennessy wear Unbridled's Song down, or would the son of Unbridled, the 1990 Kentucky Derby winner, hang on for the win? The answer was just lengths away. As the two colts drew closer to the wire, Unbridled's Song refused to give up the lead. In the end, the announcer was shouting, "And it's Unbridled's Song to win by a head!"

1

Not only had Unbridled's Song, owned by Paraneck Stable and trained by James T. Ryerson, won, he had also come close to the record time for the Breeder's Cup Juvenile.

It was only the third race in Unbridled's Song's racing career, but the colt out of Trolley Song was off to a great start. Earlier in the year, he had broken his maiden impressively, winning it by eight and a half lengths. As one announcer commented, Unbridled's Song did not only run in his maiden, he ran well.

In his second start, Unbridled's Song hadn't done so well. Critics frowned when he didn't even make the top three. But now, in the Breeder's Cup Juvenile, he had proved that he was truly one of the best. Unbridled's Song was making his mark in the racing world.

His next big win came at age three in the Florida Derby, where he beat top colt Skip Away in a romp. Fans began to wonder if Unbridled's Song would follow in his sire's footsteps and become a Kentucky Derby winner. When he took second in the Fountain of Youth Stakes, a Kentucky Derby prep race, it only increased fans' hopes for the big colt. Unbridled's Song also placed in the Peter Pan Stakes and Hutcheson Stakes.

Then, in the Wood Memorial, Unbridled's Song again surged to victory. But while doing so, he hit himself on the inside of his left forefoot, causing a quarter crack. The injury required a special bar shoe and acrylic patch. Unbridled's Song shipped to Churchill Downs in Louisville, Kentucky. There was no guarantee, only high hopes, that the injury would heal quickly enough for him to run in the 122nd Kentucky Derby.

The injury took a turn for worse, causing Unbridled's Song to show discomfort the Monday before the Kentucky Derby.

Farrier Steve Norman was summoned. The behind-the-scenes farrier became famous immediately. He was handling the hooves of the early favorite for the Kentucky Derby. After Norman removed the bar shoe and patch from Unbridled's Song's hoof, pus drained from the area. The injury hadn't been cleaned thoroughly before the patch and bar shoe were put on twelve days earlier.

Because the derby was imminent, the farrier decided to put a Z-bar shoe on Unbridled's Song. The new shoe provided support without irritating the quarter crack. The same sort of shoe was put on his other hoof to keep him better balanced. Norman's work was rewarded with a fast workout two days later. Unbridled's Song was going into the Kentucky Derby!

On the first Saturday in May, 1996, more than one hundred thousand people watched as Unbridled's Song entered the gates for the 122nd running of the Kentucky Derby. Was another victory just a mile and a quarter away? Only time - just two short minutes - would tell.

Unbridled's Song broke alertly from the gates, causing many to breathe a sigh of relief. He ran well in the race and even managed to take the lead at one point. But in the stretch, he weakened and finished a troubled fifth behind the D. Wayne Lukas-trained Grindstone. Unbridled's Song's quarter crack had bothered him. Much to the disappointment of Unbridled's Song's connections and fans, the injury would keep him out of the rest of the Triple Crown races.

Unbridled's Song took a break. The rest of the year didn't hold any big come-backs for him. His come-back came at age four. The time away from the winner's circle hadn't hurt the colt any. He had grown up some, and his color had lightened. He looked as good as ever—maybe even better than ever.

Unbridled's Song looked ready to win again as his connections aimed him for the Olympic Handicap.

Unbridled's Song was top-weighted for the Olympic Handicap. The racing world watched as he broke from the gates, ran hard, and won by a dominating three and one quarter lengths. Unbridled's Song was back.

But as it turned out, the 1997 Olympic Handicap was the last race of his career. Unbridled's Song retired as a winner to stand at Taylor Made. Unbridled's Song was to become known not only as the hero of the Breeder's Cup Juvenile and Florida Derby, but as one of the most successful sires in America and abroad.

Unbridled's Song sired winner after winner. Some of his winners included Octave, the filly who won both the 2007 Mother Goose Stakes and the 2007 Coaching Club American Oaks, and Breeders Cup Distaff winner Unbridled Elaine. He also sired the graded stakes winners Eurosilver, Domestic Dispute, Splendid Blended, Grey Song, and Political Force.

Unbridled's Song's list of winners doesn't stop there. Unbridled's Song would become the sire of one special, beautiful, gallant filly that the nation would grow to love.

Two years after Unbridled's Song retired to stud, a filly named Away started her career as a racehorse. A descendant of the great Northern Dancer, Away was by Dixieland Band, winner of the Pennsylvania Derby and Massachusetts Handicap. She was out of Be A Prospector. Away was also a descendant of the famous broodmare, La Troienne, who gave to her offspring tremendous speed. La Troienne produced fourteen foals in her lifetime, and ten of them were winners.

Away raced twice in 1999, winning once and placing once. That was only the beginning for Away. Over the next few years, Away made twenty four starts. She won seven of them, placed in four, and showed in six. Some of her best races included her win in the Minaret Stakes in 2002, and her show in the 2002 Chaposa Springs Handicap.

Away made one start at the age of six, but didn't manage to come into the money. It was time for Away to stop racing and take on a whole new career: motherhood. Away's sweet, gentle disposition would make her a wonderful dam. Away's first foal was born in 2004. The foal was by Elusive Quality, who, like Unbridled's Song, was a descendant of both Native Dancer and Mr. Prospector.

Elusive Quality and Away's colt was named Escape Route. Escape Route would go on to race and win overseas.

But Away's career as a broodmare had just begun. Away, owned by Robert Clay and Serengeti Stables, was bred for a second time. This time, she was bred to the great gray, Unbridled's Song.

Unbridled's Song and Away would become known as the sire and dam of the runner-up filly in the 134th Kentucky Derby.

On February 23, 2005, at 12:35 PM, a filly was born at Three Chimneys Farm. The bay filly was the daughter of Unbridled's Song and Away. Who would have guessed, as she stood for the first time on those long, wobbly legs, that she would become the runner-up in the Kentucky Derby?

The filly was called by her mother's name during her early life, as most Thoroughbred foals are. According to the staff at Three Chimneys, she was "just a nice baby that everyone liked." The Away filly had inherited her dam's gentle spirit. No one knew for sure at the time, but she had also inherited her sire's running heart.

-2-

"I've said it so many times and I'll say it again: she just oozed with class in everything she did."
-Jason Wells

One of the grooms in the "filly barn", Kristen Mueller, said, "She was very well put together, and the look in her eye just told you that she was special." The Away filly (also called simply: "Away") was never a "problem child" as some of the other yearlings were. If she did act up, it was only because she was feeling spunky, and even then, it was never anything serious.

Mueller added, "She was all about the game and knew her job. The main groom used to talk about how great she could be, and I was just in love with her. She could have never raced, and I still would have loved her. Little did we know, we had a superstar on our hands."

Another groom in the filly barn, Christina Morgan-Cornett, said, "I remember she was a beauty. I don't know why I took a liking to her; I just did. Maybe it was because she was taller than the other yearlings. Or maybe it was her color. Whatever it was, she caught my eye and held it."

Away loved to run from the beginning. "There are moments that just take your breath away when you are out and about on a farm," Morgan-Cornett said. "And one evening in the early spring, before the prep work really began, I remember passing the field she was in. She was out there with the other fillies, stretching her legs. They came running up a little dip, and while she was the second horse back, she easily kept pace with the others."

Morgan-Cornett added, "Looking at the filly who was leading the herd, you could tell she was running stretched out, while [the Away filly] was collected and calmly running right behind her, so effortlessly. [She] appeared to enjoy her run."

It wasn't uncommon to see Away running in her field. She did it often. "The way she ran," Morgan-Cornett remembered, "You could just tell she enjoyed it. When you watch some horses run, sometimes you can tell that's not what they're meant to do. Not with her. She enjoyed it too much."

Jason Wells was Away's main groom. For the seven months leading up to the September Keeneland sales, he cared for the tall, leggy Unbridled's Song and Away filly.

Looking back to the time when he was assigned to Away, Wells said, "...I was the odd man out and the lowest person on the totem pole, so I was given the fillies that were in the stalls furthest away from the barn office. And hers just happened to be all the way at the end of the shed row."

Wells had plenty of memories of Away to share. "The paddock she grew up in was by far the biggest of all the ones we had," Wells remembered, "and she lived out there with eight other fillies. But there was no denying who the Alpha filly was, even back then."

Away showed her potential to Wells for the first time when he was teaching her how to stand properly. While waiting to put her on the walking machine, Wells would work on getting her to place her feet correctly in preparation for the Keeneland sales.

The other fillies would fidget and move their feet nervously, but the Away filly would just stand quietly, eyes gazing off at the open hills, striking a champion's pose at a very early age. "This was when her class and character really stood out to me," Wells said, "Up until that point, I had just looked at her as one of the biggest, most awkward, but kind-eyed yearlings we had."

At around seven PM, all of the yearlings were turned out for the night. They would stay out in the paddock until about six AM the following day. Every evening, along with the eight other fillies that stayed in the paddock with her, Away would head down to what was referred to as "the big filly field." The alley leading down to the field was about 500 yards long, and that was the location for the "big filly field races." All nine fillies would line up, and whoever reached the gate first was declared the winner. Time and time again, Little Away's long-legged strides would get her to the gate in first place.

The only times she wasn't the winner, Wells remembered, were on the muddy days. The other fillies would all hurry to the field, then get down and roll in the mud. Away would watch them as if they had all gone crazy. "I've said it so many times and I'll say it again: she just oozed with class in everything she did," Wells said.

Each week, all of the yearlings would get at least one bath to get them accustomed to the things they would encounter during their lives on the track. Most of the young horses didn't tolerate bathing at first, but Away did. "She always acted like a complete lady," Wells said.

There was a secret to her good behavior, though. Away would stand perfectly still for about two or three minutes of her bath, but then she would begin to get restless. Unless, that is, you let her take the end of the hose in her mouth and let her hold it for a few seconds. It didn't matter if the hose was running or not, but letting her hold it was the only way to appease her.

Wells added, "There were several times that she would grab onto the nozzle and water would start spraying everywhere, and she would just stand there, quiet as a mouse, while gallons of water poured out the side of her mouth. And she would just look back at you as if you were the crazy one."

One of Away's trade secrets was her ability to remove her halter in the middle of the night. In the morning, when Wells went down to the field to catch her, she would be waiting at the gate halterless. "I can't even begin to tell you how many hours were spent wandering in that field in search of the missing halter," Wells said, "She had a knack for removing it in the strangest places. I can remember one point in time where it took three of us [grooms] rotating the field over the course of three days to find it."

Each day, all of the yearlings were thoroughly groomed, "to try to get their coats to gleam just a little more than they had the day before," Wells said. Away was the filly who seemed to tolerate long minutes of grooming more than the others. "I guess she knew she was the queen even back then," Wells added.

If Away did start to get excited during the groomings, Wells would talk or sing to her. "I seemed to have designated one song in particular to her one afternoon while the radio was playing," Wells said, "The song was the old Billy Joel's 'Uptown Girl'. I just couldn't believe how things would eventually play out, and I would like to think that even back then, she knew that she truly was an 'uptown girl.'"

The Away filly did everything differently than the other fillies. She almost always wanted to be first (to the paddock) to be turned out. While the other fillies paced their stalls nervously, she would lay quietly in the corner of hers. "Even the way she ate her salt block was the exact opposite from the rest of them," Wells said, "She carried herself with more class than any of the other regally bred babies we had that year, and when you looked into her eyes, you could almost tell she was destined to do something incredible."

Wells' last memory of Away was the day she got onto the truck to head to the Keeneland sales. Away traveled with one of the other fillies Wells had been caring for, a half sister to E Dubai by Storm Cat. As Wells handed Away off to the two men transporting her, he told them to "be careful, because this van has one in a million on board."

The two men looked at the Storm Cat yearling and replied, "We know all about her and have been told ten times already that this is the big horse."

Wells just looked back and said, "That's not the one I'm talking about." The two men looked to the Away filly and then back to Wells in disbelief.

"It still brings tears to my eyes to think of that memory," Wells said, "as that was the last time I saw her. But looking back on it, it truly is a priceless memory."

Away, wearing hip number 153, was to be sold September 11, 2006. Where she would go after the sale, no one knew; there would be hundreds of good yearlings at the sale. But as it happened, Away managed to catch someone's eye.

-3-

"She just had this look about her that begged me to be her owner."
- Rick Porter

Rick and Betsy Porter
Picture by Kat Cerruti

There were many racehorse owners at the September sale, but only one of them would get the Unbridled's Song and

Away filly. That man was Rick Porter, owner of Fox Hill Farm. The car dealership owner had always been a horse-racing fan. He started out as an owner by purchasing two claimers in 1994. Things snowballed from there. By the time he found Away, he owned over thirty racehorses.

Porter had already owned several champions by 2006. Among them was Rockport Harbor, sired by Unbridled's Song. Trained by John Servis, "Rocky" won all of his four starts as a two-year-old, including the Remsen and Nashua Stakes. Rockport Harbor also won the Essex Handicap as a four-year-old. He was known for his giant stride coming down the stretch.

Another of Porter's champions was the filly Round Pond, who surged to victory in the Acorn Stakes and the Breeder's Cup Distaff. Trained by Michael Matz and John Servis, Round Pond was every bit a champion. Round Pond, known around Fox Hill Farm as "The Queen," won seven of thirteen starts and was never out of the money. When Round Pond retired from racing, Porter had a new champion making his mark in the racing world.

That new champion was Hard Spun. Hard Spun, a bay colt by the three time leading sire in North America, Danzig, went on to win seven of his thirteen starts. Some of his wins would include the 2007 Lecomte Stakes, 2007 Kings Bishop Stakes, 2007 Kentucky Classic Stakes, and the 2007 Lane's End Stakes. Hard Spun was to become well known as the runner-up finisher in the 133rd Kentucky Derby. He would race second again in the Breeder's Cup Classic. Hard Spun was trained by Larry Jones, the same man who would soon train the Away filly.

Shortly after seeing Away for the first time at the Keeneland sale, Rick Porter purchased her for $375,000. Porter said, "She just had this look about her that begged me to be her owner."

Porter named the filly Eight Belles. Porter had gotten the idea for that name from the late N.C. Wyeth's (father of Andrew Wyeth, famed painter) summer home, Eight Bells. The brick home, used as a painting site by Andrew Wyeth, is located in Port Clyde, Maine.

Eight Bells is also the title of a Winslow Homer painting of 1886. N.C. Wyeth had been inspired by that painting and had also titled one of his paintings "Eight Bells." Porter had saved the name for a colt, but when he saw the gray filly, he knew the name was right for her. Porter added an "e" to the name for a feminine touch.

Eight Belles, born and raised in Kentucky, would head for a new barn in a new state. Time would tell whether or not she would become a winner.

-4-

"She had a big heart. She would do anything you asked. She would do anything for you."
-Charity Fillmore

From Keeneland, Eight Belles traveled to South Carolina, where she would be broken by Jane Dunn of Holly Hill Training Center. Eight Belles arrived at Holly Hill Training Center on September 23, 2006.

Looking back on the day she arrived, Dunn remembered, "Everything was there, but she was just big and tall and lanky. She was very leggy."

Eight Belles took to her training well. "We took a lot of time with her," Dunn said, "and we just started breezing her at her own pace. Just like a sixth grader who is six feet [tall], it takes you a while to be able to move all of that body around."

Eight Belles' exercise rider, Charity Fillmore, recalled, "She was easy as pie. She liked to go a little to the inside, but she was very well behaved. She was by far one of the easiest horses that ever came through here."

Dunn remembered Eight Belles being very business-like. "She did exactly what she was supposed to," Dunn said,

"She was a model student. She was easy to ride, she was easy to work with, she was smart ... She kind of hummed right along through the program."

Dunn never had a single problem with Eight Belles. "She was an intelligent, improving athlete," Dunn added, "She was like the kid that always does something right."

Eight Belles improved with each passing day. "She had a big heart," Fillmore said, "She would do anything you asked. She would do anything for you."

"You're never quite sure if they're that good," Dunn commented, "but if they get a little better every day and keep that up through [their] two year old and three year old years, [they] have a very good chance of being good."

After six months, on March 26, 2007, Eight Belles left Holly Hill and shipped to Aiken Training Center, where she finished her training and was evaluated by Ron Stevens.

"When she got here, a lot of adjectives were used by myself, my riders, and my grooms," Stevens said, "and they were things like 'classy', 'wow', 'athletic', and 'great mover'. We were just very impressed with her from the day she got off the van."

At Aiken Training Center, Eight Belles did a little more gait work and worked on galloping with other horses, sometimes in threes, getting a little dirt on her face and passing the other horses.

"Everything we asked her to do, she just did it with great class and caught on," Stevens said, "She was a beautiful filly to be around ... Occasionally, a few of them just stand out and you just know that they're special. And from the day she got off that van, she just had that air about her that she knew she was special."

"She was a very intelligent filly," Stevens added. "She had a great attitude. I guess I can't say enough good about her; we just loved having her here."

After three months of training, Eight Belles left Aiken Training Center; a new chapter of her life was just around the corner.

-5-

"The day she broke her maiden, I knew she was special."
- Gabriel Saez

The new chapter in Eight Belles' life began at Delaware Park in Wilmington, Delaware. Here Eight Belles would begin training with Larry and Cindy Jones.

Larry Jones, also known as the "smiling man with the cowboy hat" due to his almost always present smile, and trademark cowboy hat, entered the horse-racing industry in 1980 as an owner when he bought a $2500 claimer, a filly named Ala Turf. Ala Turf became a winner, causing Jones to look back and say, "I had a perfect record as an owner."

Jones, a former cattle farmer, took out his trainer's license in 1982. He found that training was "a whole lot more fun and exciting than farming," so he stayed with it. His wife, Cindy, became his full-time assistant.

In Jones' first year of training, he made only $3500 in earnings. The second and third years weren't much better. His breakthrough came with a stall-walking filly he owned, named Amanda Panda. Amanda Panda won a $20,000 race, and when she won again, another trainer offered $35,000 for her.

After Amanda Panda, things only got better. Josh's Madelyn, Ruby's Reception, and Wildcat Betty B were some of the stakes winners Jones trained. In 2004, Island Sand gave Jones his first grade one victory when she won the Acorn Stakes at Belmont Park.

Jones was moving up in the world of horse-racing.

When a category five tornado hit and destroyed the Joneses' longtime base of Ellis Park in 2005, they relocated to Oaklawn Park. That June, Jones received a call from Rick Porter. Porter was making a trainer change, and was wondering if Jones would take the job training for Fox Hill Farm. After some consideration, Jones decided to take it.

Jones was a hands-on trainer who often galloped his own horses so he could feel for himself how they were doing and what they were ready for. He had high standards and called for only the very best care for each horse in his barn. Honest, humble, and down-to-earth, Jones was all anyone could ask for in a trainer. He was fan-friendly, too, and never too busy to give someone a smile or handshake.

As for Cindy Jones, it was never uncommon to see her taking special time with the horses in the Jones barn, affectionately offering kisses to them and treating each horse as part of her family.

And the horses really were a part of the Jones family. Racing for Larry and Cindy Jones was all about the horses; it was never about the money or the trophies. The most important thing to the Joneses wasn't winning; it was their horses being happy, healthy, loved, and coming back to the barn safe after racing. That was what mattered most.

When Eight Belles came to Delaware Park, she didn't just become another horse in the Jones barn; she joined the Joneses' family.

Larry and Cindy Jones with Eight Belles

Picture by Candice Chavez

"She had no clue where her legs were going," Jones said much later while looking back on his first months with Eight Belles. Eight Belles was still all legs, and she couldn't seem to figure out what to do with the long things. She would change her front lead, but forget to change her back lead.

"It was all just baby stuff," Jones recalled, "She was such a tall, gangly filly, getting coordinated, growing into her body."

Eight Belles prepared to race. It wouldn't be too long before she would make her very first start.

Her first race was a Maiden Special Weight at Delaware Park. All four fillies in the race would be carrying 119 pounds. One couldn't have asked for a much nicer day for a first race. The sky was clear, the air cool, and the track fast. Eight Belles was led onto the track at odds of 1-5. On September 16, 2007, at 12:46 PM, Eight Belles made the very first start of her lifetime.

Eight Belles broke well from her position in gate three and ran well, staying toward the back of the small group of fillies. Her jockey, Mario Pino, waited patiently for the right time to make a move. That came as they were going around the far turn. Eight Belles was on the outside, running hard. Although she tried, she could not catch Christmas Dawning. Eight Belles swept beneath the wire, placing second.

But Eight Belles was still maturing. Later, Jones said, "She just needed the experience. We just let her learn the ropes." Eight Belles would learn. Perhaps not right away, but eventually, she would realize that running with all of her heart and passing beneath the wire as a winner is what it's all about.

Picture by Kat Cerruti

Eight Belles ran again at Delaware Park on October 15, 2007. The race was another Maiden Special Weight. Mario Pino was up again. This time, they would be in post position one, right on the rail. The field of seven entries was larger than the last field Eight Belles had run against.

The gates flew open. Eight Belles broke well and again settled near the back of the field. She ran a good race, making a bid for the lead coming around the turn. But she weakened in the stretch and was unable to get the win. Populist won, with Rough Water finishing second.

Perhaps she just needed a little more experience. As always, only time would tell.

On October 30, 2007, Eight Belles showed what she was made of. The race was another Maiden Special Weight at Delaware Park. Eight Belles was in post position eight for the race, and was being ridden by a different jockey.

That jockey was Gabriel Saez. Saez would play a big part in Eight Belles' life from here on. He would be the one to ride her to some of her greatest victories. Saez had started riding in Panama, where he became the leading apprentice jockey in 2005. In 2006, he moved to the United States, where he won his first race as an apprentice, as well as his first race as a journeyman.

He became a regular rider for Jones in 2006. While looking back on his first memory of Eight Belles, Saez said, "I saw her at Delaware Park for the first time. She was big and clumsy, long and thin ... She was still learning how to run. I knew Larry would get her right, and I was very excited about that."

No one imagined then that Saez would ride to a runner-up victory in the Kentucky Derby astride the same gray filly he rode in the October 30 Maiden Special Weight.

Eight Belles loaded into the gates as calmly as ever, and broke well as usual. But today, she broke fast and went straight to the lead. The announcer sounded slightly surprised as he told listeners that Eight Belles had taken the lead. Eight Belles then slowed down some, content to let another filly set the pace. Eight Belles was now running just off the pace.

All seemed to be going well as they neared the turn. As they rounded the turn, though, Eight Belles seemed to realize what was happening. This was the far turn! It was time to go down the stretch! This was where it really mattered! This was where every horse was supposed to give all she had. Eight Belles took off as though her tail was on fire. No one could catch her. As Eight Belles burned up the stretch, all the announcer could say was, "Nobody's close to Eight Belles!"

Eight Belles flew beneath the wire to win by ten lengths. "The day she broke her maiden, I knew she was special," Saez said later, "She won really easily."

For the first time, the big gray filly stood in the winner's circle. She had won money and recognition. But more than that, she had just learned what crossing the wire ahead of the others was. She had triumphed for the first time, and it would not be the last.

Picture by Kat Cerruti

Even the best lose sometimes, though, and on November 30, Eight Belles ran what was perhaps the worst race of her career. For the first time, she was running at Fair Grounds, Louisiana, rather than at Delaware Park. Fair Grounds was the Joneses' winter base, so Eight Belles had been vanned down south along with the other Jones trainees.

This was Eight Belles' first Allowance race. She was facing eight other fillies in the race and would start from position seven. Gabriel Saez was astride again.

Eight Belles broke from the gates well, but raced wide. She went wide all the way around the track and was never really a factor in the race. She finished a disappointing seventh - second to last. She was no where near the winner, Diamondaire.

But it was only Eight Belles' fourth race. There were better things to come.

It was another Allowance at Fair Grounds December 23, 2007. Gabriel Saez would be riding again, and fans had high hopes that Eight Belles would win this race.

Eight Belles stood eagerly in gate four, waiting for the gates to fly open so she could do what she now knew she was meant to do: run. The second the gates slammed open, Eight Belles shot forward, breaking well. She settled back in fifth, calmly waiting for the next move.

The race played out well for Eight Belles as the field galloped closer to the turn for home. Around the turn, Eight Belles surged forward, making her bid for the lead. She gained the lead for a moment, but Highest Class shot forward as well, catching Eight Belles. Highest Class wasn't about to give up, but neither was Eight Belles.

Eight Belles ran hard, trying for the win. But Highest Class found more speed somewhere in herself and took the win. Eight Belles placed second, but it was a good second. She had shown that she wasn't one to quit just because things were difficult. Eight Belles had shown that she had heart.

The second place finish was nothing to worry about. Her next race wasn't too far away.

-6-

"I do know she is one special filly."
- *Terry Thompson*

January 21, 2008. The new year had begun, and today, Eight Belles was running in another Allowance at Fair Grounds. Would Eight Belles lose again, or would she win? Eight Belles wore the number two saddle-cloth. Her standard white bridle stood out on her dark, salt-and-pepper (heavy on the pepper) face. Gabriel Saez sat in her saddle. For the first time, Eight Belles was racing beneath cloudy skies. The track was fast, and there were six fillies to beat.

"And they're off!" came the call as seven fillies sprang from the gates. Eight Belles stayed near the back of the group. All was going as usual. Spectators expected Eight Belles to do as she usually did - start moving up just before the turn, then try to take the lead at the top of the stretch.

That was exactly what Eight Belles did, but as it turned out, things went a little differently than usual. Eight Belles did move up just before the turn, but as the filly turned for home, she put on an amazing burst of speed. She blasted up the stretch. The race-caller, amazed, exclaimed, "Eight Belles! Look at her go!" The specators, too, were in awe as they saw Eight Belles' explosive burst of speed.

No one was coming close to Eight Belles. "Eight Belles is fleeing the scene!" The race-caller shouted excitedly as Eight Belles put more distance between herself and the other fillies. Her quick turn of foot and astonishing stretch run gave her a 15-length victory. As she swept beneath the wire, the announcer cried, "Eight Belles—wow—by double digits!" Eight Belles had started 2008 with a bang!

Her connections were all smiles in the winner's circle. When Eight Belles' quick turn of foot was mentioned, Jones joked, "She must have gotten scared of something around the quarter pole."

Earlier that day, Jones had told Porter that Eight Belles was going to run the best race of her career. But even though he had felt confident, the quality of Eight Belles' win still came as a surprise. Eight Belles was timed in 1:40:40 for a mile and forty yards, which was about as fast as a filly could run that distance at Fair Grounds.

Eight Belles had every right to be proud of herself. She had put on an incredible performance. "Larry told me she would run big," Gabriel Saez said, "And she just exploded at the top of the stretch. When she switched leads, she just won so easily!"

The fans were celebrating, too. Comments from the fans included, "Talk about an explosive turn of foot!" and "What a kick! What a professional! What a filly!"

Eight Belles was growing up. Her "big baby" phase was over, and she more than proved she had talent that day at Fair Grounds. It was the perfect way for her to start 2008.

"Hopefully this is a sign of things to come," Jones said.

Eight Belles had given fans and connections something to hope for. She would give them more and more to hope for as the weeks and months went by.

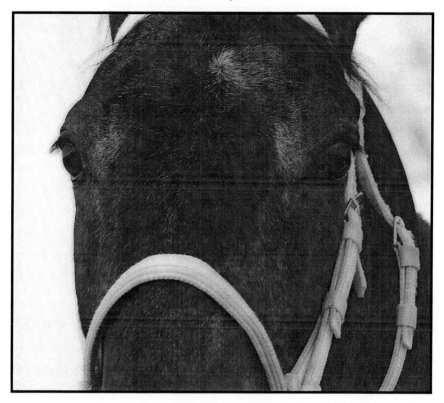

Picture by Candice Chavez

Eight Belles paraded up the track, nearing the gates. In moments, she would be running the seventh race of her career. There were seven other entries in the Martha Washington Stakes, February 17, at Oaklawn Park. This would be Eight Belles' first stakes race.

On Eight Belles' back sat a different jockey: Terry Thompson.

Eight Belles entered gate four, preparing for the break. The gates clanged open, and she surged forward, as willing and eager as ever to run her race. Eight Belles settled into the middle of the field, content to wait to make a move.

The cloudy skies made for a dreary, cool day, but in a few minutes, Eight Belles was going to make the day anything but dreary for her fans and connections. Coming around the turn, Eight Belles put on that amazing burst of speed again. She was on the outside coming around the turn, but that didn't bother her at all. The race-caller cried, "Suddenly Eight Belles explodes out to the lead!"

Explode out to the lead she did! Gray and white tail streaming out behind her, ears back in determination, Eight Belles flew up the stretch. Once again, she was romping.

The rest of the field seemed to disappear as she raced toward the wire to the music she loved: the excited roar of spectators, and the announcer yelling, "And Eight Belles, like a champion, puts six lengths on this field!"

Eight Belles wasn't quite finished. She kept right on putting distance between herself and the field. The second place finisher, Oh Lovely, didn't come anywhere near her. As she passed beneath the wire, the announcer shouted excitedly, "And Eight Belles did a phenomenal performance!"

Eight Belles had won the Martha Washington Stakes by thirteen and a half lengths.

"Don't ask me how much I had left," Terry Thompson said after the race, "I have no idea. I do know she is one special filly."

After dismounting her, Thompson told the rest of Eight Belles' connections that Eight Belles was the best horse he had ever sat on. "Larry wanted me to move around the turn,"

Thompson said, "And she did it so easily, it was like the entire field suddenly stopped. I took a long look behind us to make sure someone else wasn't making a move, but she was just pulling away from them all."

Eight Belles was blossoming into a champion.

It was Eight Belles' eigth race March 16, 2008. This was the first graded stakes race for Eight Belles: the Honeybee Stakes. Today eighth Belles would have another new jockey: Ramon Domiguez.

And today, Eight Belles was the favorite.

Eight Belles would be running against five other top fillies in this race, including the Bob Holthus-trained Pure Clan, who was wonderful as a two-year-old. Pure Clan had won both the October 28 Pocahontas (grade three) and the November 24 Golden Rod. She could very well be the main one Eight Belles needed to beat.

The gates burst open. Six fillies leapt from the gates. Many eyes were on number six, the gray filly, who settled back in third. Eight Belles ran her race well, waiting, then making her move at the turn. Coming around the turn, she went for the lead. So did Pure Clan, but Pure Clan was no match for Eight Belles.

Eight Belles was hand-ridden down the stretch, and she raced beneath the wire to win by an easy length and a half, leaving the race-caller shouting in excitement, "And it's a superstar in the making!"

As Eight Belles entered the winner's circle, the race-caller said, "You may be looking at the best three-year-old in America."

The thought alone was more than a little exciting. Eight Belles was certainly turning into a superstar, and the words "Kentucky Oaks" and "Kentucky Derby" were now being mentioned, together with the name "Eight Belles."

Eight Belles' connections were faced with a decision. What race would be best for Eight Belles next? There was the Fantasy Stakes, where Eight Belles could face fillies again. But there was also the Arkansas Derby, where Eight Belles could run against the colts.

Eight Belles' connections considered their choices carefully.

Which race would they choose? Fans waited impatiently, eager to know where the ultra-talented filly would run next.

-7-

" She showed a lot of heart."
- Rick Porter

Owner and trainer decided that the Fantasy Stakes would be Eight Belles' next start. Eight Belles was going to face off with Pure Clan again. Most racing fans assumed that Pure Clan would be Eight Belles' main challenger. Eight Belles would also be up against the Steve Asmussen trainee, Alina. Alina was coming off of an eighteen and a half length victory in the March Green Oaks Stakes. One other filly, French Kiss, would also be running in the Fantasy.

On March 31, Eight Belles had her final work-out for the Fantasy, Terry Thompson astride. Thompson told Jones that Eight Belles wasn't even blowing afterwards.

Eight Belles was ready to race in the Fantasy. Fans eagerly waited for the race. Anticipation grew when Jones and Porter said they planned to leave the door ajar for the Kentucky Derby.

As the day for the Fantasy drew near, fans grew more and more excited. Would Eight Belles romp again, defeating

Pure Clan, Alina, and French Kiss by several lengths? Or would she be defeated, crushing the dreams of a filly going to the Kentucky Derby?

The answer was just days away.

The day for the Fantasy Stakes, April 6, dawned clear and mild at Oaklawn Park. Eight Belles had drawn post position three. She would be right between Alina, number four, and Pure Clan, number two.

Spectators watched anxiously as the favorite, Eight Belles, entered the gates. Her jockey would again be Ramon Dominguez. The track condition was fast, the odds in her favor. But anything could happen. The gates flew open, and for the first time, Eight Belles did not break perfectly: She broke in the air. Alina took the lead from the start and stayed there, setting a modest pace.

Eight Belles' fans groaned as Eight Belles ran near the back of the field. Had the less-than-perfect break cost Eight Belles the race? She had never broken badly before, after all. The field of four galloped on around the track. Eight Belles dropped behind the other three fillies after a quarter-mile. Perhaps this was where viewers and spectators realized it would not be an easy race for Eight Belles.

As they neared the far turn, Eight Belles tried to regain her form, running three-wide. She nearly gained the lead at the three-quarter pole, but Alina had more to give. Alina now had the lead by two lengths. Eight Belles chased after her. Both fillies gave it all they had as they battled down the stretch. For the first time in three races, Eight Belles was being challenged by another filly. Spectators roared, many of them cheering for Eight Belles, others for Alina. Some cheered just because they were loving the two-horse race down the stretch.

Some people were convinced Eight Belles was going to lose, and that even her heart wouldn't carry her beneath the wire in first place. Others were sure Eight Belles could and would take the win. She had a lot of heart; she was determined. Surely a bad break from the gates and a fight down the stretch would not cost her the race.

It looked like history repeating itself as Alina and Eight Belles fought their way down the stretch. Eight Belles was running with Alina much like her sire had run against Hennessy many years before, in the Breeder's Cup Juvenile.

Eight Belles refused to lose the Fantasy. She stole the lead from Alina, and, giving a brilliant effort, hit the wire in the lead by a neck.

Spectators cheered. Fans from all over the country, who had been watching the race on television, leapt to their feet in excitement. It was Eight Belles! The race caller shouted, "Here's Eight Belles! A surge at the wire!" It had been the toughest race Eight Belles had run, but she had won it.

"Through the stretch, she just kept driving," Ramon Dominguez said.

Alina took the place, and Pure Clan, who, surprisingly, had not been the main challenger for Eight Belles, took the show. Eight Belles paraded around the winner's circle to the cheers of fans and connections.

"...She showed a lot of heart," Porter said after the race, "I'm tickled pink to get out of here with a 'W.'"

Fans agreed. Eight Belles had definitely shown that she had a lot of heart. If anyone had doubted it before, they had no reason to doubt it now. But had Eight Belles run well enough to go to the Kentucky Derby? Headlines after the Fantasy read: "Eight Belles Could Run in Derby" and "Eight Belles Derby-Bound?" It was the question many were asking. When asked about it, Porter said, "We have four weeks. A lot can happen in four weeks."

In other words, nothing was for sure.

Picture by Candice Chavez

The next two weeks were full of mixed feelings. There was hope – hope that Eight Belles would run in the derby and get a chance at becoming the first filly to win it since Winning

Colors in 1988. There was doubt. Would a filly really challenge nineteen top colts on May 3, 2008?

Fans weren't sure what they wanted. If Eight Belles went to the Oaks, some were convinced she would romp, then go on to race in the Preakness against the boys. Others thought Eight Belles should go to the Derby, that she deserved the chance to win it. Others had no idea what to think. After all, it's not every year that a filly is considered for the Kentucky Derby!

Eight Belles' connections weren't certain yet either. Eight Belles had been nominated for the Triple Crown races, but there was no guarantee that she would run in any of them. Eight Belles shipped to Keeneland, in Lexington, Kentucky, where she would train for the Kentucky Oaks along with her stablemate, Proud Spell, who was owned by Brereton Jones (no relation to Larry Jones).

Porter told reporters and fans, "We know [Eight Belles] will get the distance [of the Kentucky Derby], number one, and we know she has a lot of heart. She can run on the front, she can stalk, and she can come from off the pace. She's a very talented filly ... We think she belongs and can compete with colts at the very top end."

Eight Belles' earnings of $308,650 put her among the top twenty horses on the Kentucky Derby graded earnings list.

When asked about the decision on whether or not Eight Belles would run in the Kentucky Derby, Jones said, "It's a day to day thing. No decision has been made."

Fans practically held their breath, waiting to know where the filly would run next.

-8-

On April 20, both Eight Belles and Proud Spell, who also was nominated for the Triple Crown races, worked for a half mile at Keeneland.

"We just wanted to stretch their legs," Cindy Jones said. But Eight Belles had a little more in mind than just stretching her legs. With Gabriel Saez riding, Eight Belles went a half mile in :46.60, second fastest of 39 works at the distance. Eight Belles was ready to go!

The plans called for Eight Belles and Proud Spell to ship (on April 25) to Churchill Downs, home of the run for the roses (the Kentucky Derby) and the run for the lillies (the Kentucky Oaks). But beyond that?

"We don't know," Cindy Jones said when asked about where the fillies would run next. "The decision will be made at entry time."

The fillies' next starts continued to be up in the air for the next few days. Jones preferred to keep Eight Belles and Proud Spell separate at this point in their careers.

Eight Belles' connections decided that if Eight Belles drew a poor position in the Derby, she would go to the Kentucky Oaks. "She doesn't get out of the gate real fast," Porter said, "and in a twenty horse field, if she happens to draw the outside post position, she'll be at a great disadvantage going into the first turn."

But if Eight Belles drew a poor position in the Oaks and a good one in the Kentucky Derby, she would run for the roses. Jones said that he would consider a bad post position in the Oaks a sign from above to go ahead and run her in the Kentucky Derby.

The drawing for the Oaks was on April 29. Proud Spell got post position eight. Although she had been nominated for the Triple Crown races, Proud Spell was now a confirmed Oaks starter. Eight Belles drew the outside, twelve, for the Oaks. "It looks like we got our sign on where we are going to run," Jones said with a laugh.

Porter told fans and the media, "It will take a very bad draw to keep us out of the Derby."

Eight Belles drew the sixth selection for the Kentucky Derby. It was the sign from above that Jones was looking for, and it secured the good post position everyone had hoped for.

It was official. Eight Belles would run against nineteen colts on May 3, 2008. And maybe, just maybe, she would cross the wire ahead of them all. Just maybe she would be the one to have the blanket of roses draped over her shoulders. Fans dared to hope as they cheered in excitement. Eight Belles, a filly, was going to the Derby!

The trainer of Kentucky Derby-winning filly Winning Colors, D. Wayne Lukas, thought Eight Belles had a chance for the win in the Derby. Lukas told Jones that he thought one of Winning Colors' advantages had been her large size. Eight Belles would have the same advantage. Although she wasn't heavily built, Eight Belles was tall. Matching up with the boys structurally would be an important asset when Eight Belles ran in the Derby.

Having had nine starts, Eight Belles also had more experience than any of the other horses going into the derby. That was especially impressive because she had won all of her four starts in 2008. Three of them she had won with ease.

Perhaps Eight Belles would join the list of Derby winners. After all, she might follow in her grandsire's footsteps. Unbridled had won the Kentucky Derby by three and a half lengths.

The next step for Eight Belles' connections would be to choose jockeys for Proud Spell and Eight Belles. Jones chose Gabriel Saez to ride both. Porter never questioned the decision, and said he was one hundred percent behind the choice. This would be Saez's first Oaks as well as his first Derby. What a weekend it would be if he won both races!

Jones would also become the first trainer to win the Oaks and Derby back to back with fillies, if Eight Belles and Proud Spell did prove to be the best of the best. As the Derby got closer, Eight Belles and Proud Spell prepared to run the most important races they had ever run. The bay (Proud Spell) and the gray (Eight Belles) were going to run on Derby weekend!

Eight Belles became the thirty-ninth filly to run in the Kentucky Derby. The first fillies ever to run in the Kentucky Derby were Gold Mine and Ascension. They both entered the 1874 Kentucky Derby. Gold Mine finished fifteenth; Ascension finished tenth.

Over the years, other fillies had run against the boys in the Kentucky Derby. But none of them came into the money ... until 1906. In 1906, a filly named Lady Navarre entered the run for the roses. Lady Navarre made history when she finished second. In fact, if Eight Belles ended up running second, she would be the first filly to finish second in the run for the roses since Lady Navarre.

If Eight Belles won the roses, she would become only the fourth filly in thoroughbred-racing history to do so. The first filly to win the Kentucky Derby was Regret in 1915. Regret led the way through much of the race, then drew away from the field at the stretch. She passed beneath the wire in the lead and easing up.

After Regret, it was the Leroy Jolley trainee, Genuine Risk, who became a filly Derby winner. The bright chestnut filly surged to a stunning, exciting victory in the 1980 Kentucky Derby. Genuine Risk not only won the Kentucky Derby, but was in the money for the rest of the Triple Crown races as well.

The next filly to win the Kentucky Derby was Winning Colors. She raced beneath the wire to win in 1988. Winning Colors was also the first Kentucky Derby winner to go wire to wire (to stay in the lead for the whole race). But Winning Colors was the last filly to stand in the winner's circle with the blanket of roses over her back. In twenty long years, no filly had crossed the wire in first place at the Kentucky Derby.

Other fillies had run in the Derby since Winning Colors, but none of them had come into the top three. No filly had entered the Derby since 1999, when Excellent Meeting and Three Ring both stepped up to challenge the boys. Three Ring finished a disappointing nineteenth, and Excellent Meeting, the favorite, finished fifth.

List of Fillies in the Kentucky Derby

(those that came into the money are in italics; those that won are in bold italics)

Year	Name	Finish
1875	Gold Mine	15th
1875	Ascension	10th
1876	Marie Michon	7th
1876	Lizzie Stone	6th
1877	Early Light	8th
1879	Wissahickon	9th
1879	Ada Glenn	7th
1883	Pike's Pride	6th
1906	*Lady Navarre*	*2nd*
1911	Round the World	6th
1912	*Flamma*	*3rd*
1913	*Gowell*	*3rd*
1914	Watermelon	7th
1914	*Bronzewing*	*3rd*
1915	***Regret***	***1st***
1918	*Viva America*	*3rd*

1919	Regalo	9th
1920	Cleopatra	15th
1921	Careful	5th
1921	*Prudery*	*3rd*
1922	Startle	8th
1929	Ben Machree	18th
1930	Alcibiades	10th
1932	Oscillation	13th
1934	Bazarr	9th
1934	Mata Hari	4th
1935	Nellie Flag	4th
1936	Gold Seeker	9th
1945	Misweet	12th
1959	Silver Spoon	5th
1980	***Genuine Risk***	***1st***
1982	Cupecoy's Joy	10th
1984	Althea	19th
1984	Life's Magic	8th
1988	***Winning Colors***	***1st***
1995	Serena's Song	19th
1999	Three Ring	19th
1999	Excellent Meeting	5th

Perhaps Eight Belles would be the next filly to make history by beating the colts. Maybe, just maybe, it was possible.

-9-

"Hello? Larry to Eight Belles!"
-Larry Jones

It poured on the day of the Kentucky Oaks. The track turned to slop. No amount of work done by the maintenance crew could keep the mud well under control. The Joneses saddled up their bay filly for the Kentucky Oaks under a rainy, dark sky. The call to post rang out loud and clear. Despite the dreary weather, about one hundred thousand people had shown up for the 134th running of the Oaks.

Proud Spell entered gate eight. Gabriel Saez sat in her saddle, wearing Brereton Jones' orange and green silks. Pure Clan was in this race - the same filly who had raced against Eight Belles in both the Honeybee and Fantasy. Eleven fillies broke from the gates at the same instant.

Proud Spell settled in just off the pace, a perfect position to be in. Mud flew in all directions as the fillies ran through it. Coming around the far turn, Proud Spell and Saez made their move. Proud Spell, slinging mud in the faces of the other fillies, took off up the homestretch. There was no catching Proud Spell.

Proud Spell flew beneath the wire, winning the Kentucky Oaks. Covered in mud, but looking every bit a winner, Proud Spell had the blanket of pink lillies draped over her back. Brereton Jones and Larry Jones were all smiles as they stood in the muddy winner's circle. Cindy Jones, along with Corey York - the main groom for both Eight Belles and Proud Spell, led Proud Spell around as the crowd cheered. The rain and slop didn't matter any more.

The Kentucky Oaks was over, and the Kentucky Derby was just ahead.

People all over the country turned on their televisions to see the ESPN special of Eight Belles' replayed pre-Derby workout. With Jones astride, she had breezed Thursday morning. Jeannine Edwards, news reporter for ESPN, had ridden with Jones throughout his ride on Eight Belles to give viewers a closer look at the filly who would run for the roses.

Eight Belles paraded up the track, ears up in curiosity and anticipation. Jones let her inspect the stall she would be in just before the Derby. Eight Belles took it all in stride, looking interested but not worried over the new surroundings. Fans cheered as Eight Belles walked past them, looking every bit the "superstar-in-the-making" she was. Then came the moment everyone was waiting for. Jones turned Eight Belles counter-clockwise around the track, and let her out.

Viewers smiled, watching the brilliant filly gallop around the track. Eight Belles made running look easy and fun. Even the lead change she did looked almost effortless. Jones leaned back a little. It was time to pull up. Jones tugged at the bit, asking Eight Belles to slow down. Eight Belles' ears flicked back and forth. Viewers laughed with delight and amusement. Eight Belles was listening, but it was obvious that she didn't plan on obeying.

"Hello? Larry to Eight Belles!" Jones called. Viewers laughed harder. Of all of the pre-Derby clips, this was something no one had seen before. Much to viewers' amusement, Eight Belles did decide to slow down after Jones called to her. She eased back to a canter, and was rewarded with Jones' "That's it, sweetheart."

The special, one-of-a-kind ride was seen by thousands of people across the country. Eight Belles had captured even more hearts. It was while watching her replayed workout that some people suddenly made up their minds to root for the steel gray filly. She was the girl going up against the boys. She could be about to make history.

With over one hundred and fifty thousand people piling into Louisville, Kentucky for the 134th running of the run for the roses, it was wondered if Eight Belles would shine on Derby day, or fail in the test of champions.

Picture by Candice Chavez

Kentucky Derby morning dawned sunny and mild. The breeze worked to help the maintenance crew dry the track. It looked like there would be a good, fast track for the 134th Kentucky Derby.

All was well in Barn 43, where the Joneses' two fillies were. Proud Spell, the Oaks winner, was being photographed by reporters. Buddy, the Joneses' African Gray parrot, was whistling outside his cage. It was a good way to begin Kentucky Derby morning.

Eight Belles stood in her stall, gray head sticking out over the door. She was waiting patiently for her chance to run.

With the hustle and bustle around her, Eight Belles probably guessed what was coming. She was going to race again, and she was going to give it everything she had.

Already, Churchill Downs was filling up with people who had come to watch the Derby.

Fancy hats and dresses were everywhere. Some hats were beautiful, others wild. Bettors were already lining up at the betting windows, ready to bet on whichever horse they expected to win. Eight Belles was the fourth choice at odds of 13-1. Big Brown, the early favorite, remained the favorite even though he would be starting from post position twenty. Pyro and Colonel John were the second and third choices.

Cameras were clicking everywhere. Reporters could be seen all over the track grounds. The infield was starting to fill up. People around the country were preparing to turn on their televisions, eager to watch the Derby and the races on the Derby undercard from their own homes. The Kentucky Derby was getting underway!

-10-

"The filly's right there with a fighting chance!"-race-caller Tom Durkin during the 134th Kentucky Derby

Excitement grew as the twenty Kentucky Derby entries prepared for the walk-over. They would leave the backside of the track and head for the saddling paddock. One fan remembered standing there, taking pictures of the entries, when a gray backside appeared in his camera lens. That big gray was Eight Belles. She was confident, and, as one fan put it "more intimidating than any filly I had seen in a long time."

Eight Belles received more applause and cheers than any of the entries as she walked through the "tunnel" of cheering people on the backside. Eight Belles took all of the commotion in stride, looking every bit the lady she was.

"It was obvious Eight Belles [became] an instant favorite," one fan said. "She and Larry Jones really stood out from the rest during the walk-over and captured a lot of casual fans just from that moment."

After seeing her in the walk-over, many respected her much more than they ever had in the past. She looked like a serious contender, and perhaps, in minutes, she would prove that she certainly was.

Excitement rippled through the crowd like electricity as the moment everyone was waiting for drew closer. Then came the call: "Rider's UP!" Trainers who had been carefully saddling their horses, preparing them for the race ahead, moved to boost their chosen jockeys into the saddle. One by one, the Derby entries walked out of their stalls.

134th Kentucky Derby, 2008
Entries with Trainers and Jockeys

Entry	Trainer	Jockey
Cool Coal Man	Nick Zito	Julien Leparoux
Tale of Ekati	Barclay Tagg	Eibar Coa
Anak Nakal	Nick Zito	Rafael Bejarano
Court Vision	Bill Mott	Garrett Gomez
Eight Belles	Larry Jones	Gabriel Saez
Z Fortune	Steve Asmussen	Robby Albarado
Big Truck	Barclay Tagg	Javier Castellano
Visionaire	Michael Matz	Jose Lezcano
Pyro	Steve Asmussen	Shaun Bridgmohan
Colonel John	Eoin Harty	Corey Nakatani

Entry	Trainer	Jockey
Z Humor	Bill Mott	Rene Douglass
Smooth Air	Bennie Stutts, Jr.	Manoel Cruz
Bob Black Jack	James Kasparoff	Richard Migliore
Monba	Todd Pletcher	Ramon Dominguez
Adriano	Graham Motion	Edgar Prado
Denis of Cork	David Carroll	Calvin Borel
Cowboy Cal	Todd Pletcher	John Velazquez
Recapturetheglory	Louie Roussell	E. T. Baird
Gayego	Paulo Lobo	Mike Smith
Big Brown	Rick Dutrow, Jr.	Kent Desormeaux

Eight Belles, led by Larry Jones on one side and her groom, Corey York, on the other, walked calmly around the paddock. The Gray Miss was as poised and easy-going as ever. Many were rooting for the filly by now. To see a filly win would be beyond thrilling.

As Eight Belles walked the paddock, she looked at the excited people around her. Jones said four months later, "She knew everyone was [there] for her and she just decided that with 150,000 people looking, she felt she owed it to every one of them to make eye contact. I think people were mesmerized by her."

And a lot of people were. There was something about Eight Belles that made people look twice, and sometimes not stop looking. Some would say it was her steel gray color. Others would say it was her size. Most would agree, though, that it was her sweet nature and quiet dignity that turned heads. She wasn't jigging or nervous. She was simply interested in the goings-on around her. She was a perfect contender for the run for the roses. Eight Belles was ready to go.

Eight Belles was led through the tunnel and out to the track as the call to post sounded. Clear notes rang out over Churchill Downs, calling twenty horses to post for the run for the roses. Jones patted Eight Belles' neck and released her lead into the hands of the pony rider. The singing of "My Old Kentucky Home" began. The crowd joined in to sing Kentucky's state song as twenty top three-year-olds paraded onto the track.

The heat, the long day – none of it mattered anymore as everyone concentrated on one thing: the Kentucky Derby. As the last note of "My Old Kentucky Home" died away, a roar went up from the crowd. Eight Belles walked beside her lead pony, looking at her surroundings with pricked ears.

The first filly to enter the derby in nine years broke into a canter, heading for gate five.

Eight Belles, along with her rivals, reached the starting gates. Excited cheers went up. Eight Belles, being her usual lady-like self, loaded into the gates without a problem. Saez readied for the break. Eight Belles stared out of the gates at the track before her.

For the first time in her life, she was about to run for a mile and a quarter. For the first time, she was going to run against the boys. For the first time, she was going to run in Kentucky, the land where she was born. No one will ever know for sure what went on in that pretty gray head as Eight Belles waited for the rest of the Derby entries to load.

Perhaps she made up her mind to run her heart out. Or maybe she was just thinking of how much fun it would be to fly over a track again. Just maybe, she decided to run hard against the boys, no matter how big or talented they might be.

There was a moment of near silence as the last horse, Big Brown, entered the gates. The voice of race-caller Tom Durkin came over the loudspeakers: "They're in the gate."

The race, the 134th running of the Kentucky Derby, began in all its glory as the gates clanged open. Twenty horses sprang forward to the thrilled, excited roar of thousands. Durkin cried, "And they're off in the Kentucky Derby!" Eight Belles broke well, moving for a spot near the rail. Bob Black Jack put on an early burst of speed, taking the lead. Eight Belles raced behind him for a moment, then dropped back, settling in behind the front runners. The most amazing race of her life had just begun.

Eight Belles was off to good start as they raced up the first stretch of track.

Rounding the first turn, Eight Belles was in tight traffic. Cowboy Cal, Recapturetheglory, and Cool Coal Man were all close to her. Bob Black Jack continued to lead the way. Eight Belles picked up her speed a bit, going from fifth to fourth, running well despite the lack of running room.

The crowd's cheers grew a bit louder as the horses rounded the next turn. The greatest two minutes in horse-racing were almost over. Durkin's voice became excited as he said, "The filly's right there with a fighting chance!" In seconds, Kentucky would have her Derby winner. The crowd rose to their feet. The final turn was coming! As the horses rounded the final turn, Big Brown shot out to the lead. Eight Belles chased after him.

The roar of the crowd was deafening. Over one hundred and fifty-five thousand people were on their feet, screaming at the top of their lungs for the horses surging down the stretch. Eight Belles was not giving up. The announcer was going wild. "The game filly Eight Belles trying to run [Big Brown] down in the final furlong!" With every stride, Eight Belles kept from dropping too far behind Big Brown, who was just lengths ahead.

The rest of the field fell back. The nearest colt behind Eight Belles was Denis of Cork, and he was three and a half lengths back. Running with all of the big heart she had shown throughout her short life, Eight Belles flew beneath the wire. She was only four and three-quarter lengths behind the winner, Big Brown.

An earth-shaking roar went up from the spectators. Eight Belles put her ears up. In her young mind, she may have known that much of the roar was for her. She was only the second filly in Kentucky Derby history to finish second in the run for the roses – the first filly to finish second in 102 years. It had been a strong, courageous finish – a finish to be proud of. She had beaten eighteen colts. She hadn't let the winner get too far ahead of her. Yes, the crowd was roaring as much for her as they were for the winning colt.

Up in the grandstands, Eight Belles' connections were high-fiving excitedly, thrilled over their filly's gallant Derby run. She had done all of them proud.

Eight Belles had made history. Even though she hadn't swept beneath the wire in the lead, she had given spectators and viewers something breath-taking to watch. All of the glory and beauty of her runner-up victory amazed and thrilled those watching. Eight Belles had finished the race, and she had finished it with all of the heart, spirit, beauty, determination, courage, and grace she possessed. She had finished like a champion. In just a few minutes, Eight Belles had won more than most horses win in a lifetime.

She had won the love, admiration, and respect of a nation. Eight Belles galloped out, ending her race in glory. And then ... she galloped out of our lives.

Picture by Candice Chavez

Eight Belles broke down a quarter-mile after the wire. In one stride, she suffered compound fractures of both ankles (at the fetlock joints) and collapsed in front of the outrider. The catastrophic injuries were beyond repair; there was no way to save her. Much to the devastation of her connections and to the grief of her many fans, Eight Belles, runner up in the 134th Kentucky Derby, was euthanized on the track. The loss was heart-breaking.

-11-

"For Eight Belles: He could have had any ... He chose the best."
-Bloodhorse Memory Wall

People all over the country mourned Eight Belles' breakdown. So many people had been touched by Eight Belles' life and death. One woman said that she had been devastated after the breakdown, but had gone outside and seen two beautiful rainbows splashed across the sky. She took that as a sign that Eight Belles was all right.

Another woman said that she had asked God to show her Eight Belles was safe. When she developed some pictures, she found one she had forgotten about. It was a picture of Eight Belles during the post parade, and in the picture, the woman found the sign she was looking for. During the post parade, a ray of light had rested on Eight Belles' gray head for a moment. Though it had only lasted for a few seconds, it shone long enough to be captured in a picture. The woman felt like that was a sign from above, and as she looked at it she felt that God told her, "I was with her that day, and she is with Me now. It was My plan, and she is at peace."

Larry Jones, too, had a story to tell. Staying in a motel while waiting to move into a new house in Delaware, Jones knelt with a Bible on his lap. It was there that he cried out in prayer, while a bad thunderstorm was going on outside. Jones, in tears, asked God why his filly had been taken.

As Jones prayed, a huge clap of thunder sounded above. In that thunder clap, Jones felt that God told him, "She wasn't your filly, she was My filly, and she still is."

Jones said, "I keep looking in [Eight Belles'] stall and she [isn't] there, so, yeah, I know she's not coming back. Maybe God thought we had her good and ready for Him. I have a lot of faith in that. He's going to use this for good things somehow. I don't know what it is or why He had to do it this way, but one thing is for sure: God does not make mistakes. There is a reason for this."

People all over the nation wondered what good things could come of such a tragedy as they, along with Eight Belles' connections, tearfully tried to move forward.

Eight Belles, through her life and death, touched hearts like few horses have ever done before. There was something special - very special - about Eight Belles. One fan, who had been on the backside after her breakdown, said that they (those on the backside) first heard it was Pyro who had gone down. Next, they heard it was Denis of Cork. While either colt going down would have been tragic, the incredible shock and sadness came when someone finally blurted, "It was the filly." It was the filly who had captured the love of so many, and it was the filly who had just put on the performance of a lifetime. Why she had gone down, no one could understand.

Veterinarians were puzzled over the breakdown. It was the first fatal breakdown recorded in Kentucky Derby history. Eight Belles' necropsy results, released two weeks later, revealed no pre-existing bone abnormalities. Eight Belles also tested negative for all banned substances and steroids. The reason for her sudden collapse remains uncertain. Jones said a mis-step may have been to blame. Breakdowns just don't occur where and when Eight Belles' did. She collapsed at the seven-eighths pole, while happily galloping out. As Jones put it, "It's not supposed to end that way."

No one could stop thinking about Eight Belles. While some focused on trying to figure out why exactly the breakdown had happened, others searched for ways to honor her, and for ways to show how much the gray filly had really won.

One of the many tributes to Eight Belles was the Eight Belles Memory Wall created by Bloodhorse. The online memory wall was signed 444 times by people wanting to express how much Eight Belles meant to them, how much they had loved her, how special she had been, and how much she is missed.

[Copyright Blood-Horse Publications. Reprinted with permission of copyright owner.]

"You gave us such a thrill. You gave us your all ... we will forever keep you in our hearts. Godspeed, Belle." -Laura

"Eight Belles was such a beautiful filly. She was outstanding in the Derby running her heart out and beating 18 males. For a

few precious seconds, I almost dreamed she'd catch the big guy. No matter. She is a true champion .... RIP, sweet girl." - Lexie C

"May there be a field of sweet clover in Heaven for her." - Sharon

"She was such a gorgeous filly. I will never forget cheering out loud, "She's going to come in second!!!!!" I will never, never forget Eight Belles." - Melissa

"She was beautiful, poised beyond her years, and had the heart of a champion ... Belle, you will live on in all of our memories, and your spirit runs free. Rest in peace." - Cee

"Nearing the end of the Derby, it was obvious that Big Brown was going to win ... however, I was just as excited to see Eight Belles coming through the pack and taking over second; we were all yelling, 'Look, the filly's going to be second!' As she crossed the line, she was running gamely with her ears pricked, doing what she loved doing: being a racehorse. That's how I will always remember Eight Belles. Rest in peace, sweet girl; you will never be forgotten."- Richie

"What great things can be said about Eight Belles that haven't been said already? You gave us your all, your life, and I'll never forget seeing you fly down the stretch, 18 boys in your wake. Run in peace." - Caitlin

"The Kentucky sky will forever shine a little brighter because her star has joined the Ages. And while we are poorer for this great loss, we are richer for having known her in the first place. Run freely in the light, gallant, darling girl. We will never forget your noble heart..." - Team Ivytree

"Beautiful Belles, you had an amazing spirit ... You crossed the wire ahead of the best three-year-olds in the country with your ears up, begging to go farther. You proved you belonged in the toughest race there is, and that you loved every second of it. I don't

know why this had to happen to you, but I know that somehow, somewhere, you're still running with your ears up. Rest in peace, darling." - Natalie

"Eight Belles went out the way she would have wanted to. Yes, too early, but she gave her life to show the world just what kind of heart she had ... All I can say, Eight Belles, is thank you for making me fall in love with you and the greatest sport in the world. I can't wait to see you again someday." - Travis

"You are what this sport is about and you old girl [were] all heart and class. We will tell our grandchildren about the unbelievable effort Saturday. And you, Eight Belles, will live forever a champion." - Fred B

"We will miss you, dear filly. You can run like the wind on the wings of angels now." - JJ

"Goodbye, beautiful Belles; the world lost a champion filly, but Heaven welcomed a new star!" - Laura

"...I do find comfort in knowing she died doing what she loved to do: run, run, run ... RIP, beautiful girl, rest in peace ... you are amazing and made a large statement in your short time on earth!" - Bob Q.

"Thank you, Eight Belles, for allowing so many of us to witness greatness. RIP, beautiful girl." - Morgan

"She was gorgeous and a real champion ... She was something, that Eight Belles, she was really something." - Theresa Lyn

"...She will be remembered as the horse with the most heart that day, and [she] showed that girls rule! God will most certainly bless Eight Belles." - Colleen

"*Eight Belles: Run fast and free with all the other great ones in equine heaven. You ran a great race in the Derby and belonged there. You are loved and missed.*" - Lisa

"*...Goodbye, Eight Belles ... magnificent job; well done.*" - Pam

"*...I just wanted to tell you, Eight Belles, you looked absolutely stunning in the Derby. Thanks for being my hero! Rest in peace.*" - Thomas

"*Beautiful filly, I was awed by your glorious presence as you trotted along the track just days before a tragedy that shook our world. I will never forget the glow of health and contentment that radiated from your powerful frame. You, Eight Belles, were the real deal, a Champion. You will never be forgotten.*" - Jeanne

"*For Belles: She's going home, He could have any ... He chose the best.*" - Terry

"*Eight Belles, so many people love and miss you! You were truly amazing and I will always remember you! I'm sure you are in an amazing place right now! You really did go out in glory, doing something you truly loved. RIP, Eight Belles! I love you!*" - Lauren

"*Eight Belles, you were so beautiful and I am very proud of your magnificent accomplishments. I know that you are in Heaven enjoying your roses. You'll never be forgotten.*" - Tracy

"*We may never truly know just how far you would have [gone] in your racing career, but we do know that your impact on mankind will not be forgotten. Your legacy is in history forever, Eight Belles. And every time the thunder roars, I will know that you are up in heaven, racing the champions, and leaving dirt in their faces.*" - Teresa

"What a true lady Eight Belles was ... Bless your heart, Belle, and thank you for taking all of us on a spectacular ride." - Amy

"...Race on, Eight Belles, Heaven's winning post awaits you." - Maggie

"God comes to earth every day and picks the most beautiful flowers for His garden in heaven; Eight Belles was the most beautiful Rose on Derby day ... and she got picked." - Coco

Picture by Candice Chavez

-12-

"They say that you have to have heart. Never saw more in my life!"
-Eight Bells for Eight Belles Petition

The phrase "eight bells" notes the ending of one watch and the beginning of another on a ship. Horse-lover Joni Massengale created an online petition, requesting that the bells be rung eight times at the 135th Kentucky Derby in honor of Eight Belles. The petition said that Eight Belles "raced with the heart of a champion and a spirit greater than her body".

The website created by Massengale, <u>8bellsforeightbelles. org</u>, allowed people to sign up in support of the petition and leave comments.

Massengale created an intro for the site. To the audio of eight bells ringing, the words "Spirit ... Courage ... Hope ... Beauty ... Heart ... Grace ... Determination ...Champion ... EIGHT BELLES" flashed up. The words perfectly described what Eight Belles had shown during her life.

Within days, the petition had been signed by five thousand people. When Rick Porter mentioned Massengale's website in an interview, the 8bellsforeightbelles petition signatures grew at an even faster rate. In just weeks, the petition had over ten thousand signatures. The comments and signatures came from people all over the world.

"You will always be in my heart and soul. Your courage and heart were second to none. You were a true champion in every sense of the word and I will always love you." - J. Palmer, Landsdale, PA

"God bless you, Eight Belles. We were blessed with your presence for such a brief time but your memory forever!" - M. Whitney, West Columbia, SC

"Any horse with that much heart deserves to be remembered!" - L. Lilly, Jasper, IN

"You are my favorite horse. You are still running races in my room with my other toy horses. I love you." - K. Jackson (age 7), Georgetown, KY

"...her brilliance and her heart will be remembered forever. Even as I am writing this, my heart is full for her." - E. Phillips, Miles City, MT

"Beauty, grace, heart, courage, and valor [were] what she showed, may her memory live forever in every horseman." - E. Karugu, Nakuru, Bahrain

"I have seen all of her races. She was a true Champion. She passed away doing what she was born and bred to do: run very, very fast. She proved that she deserved to run with the Colts. She may not have won the race, but she was clearly the Best of the Rest." - D. Isken, Wilmington, DE

"You will always be in my family's heart, Eight Belles. You were absolutely beautiful. It was the first time my 5-year-old daughter watched the Derby and she thought it was so great that your

number was number five! We are so proud of you ..." - D. Van Horn, Ashland, Ohio

"Eight Belles, I cheered for you from the beginning of the race. When I saw you made it to second place, I was THRILLED ... then my heart broke ... The heavenly pastures are blessed with another Champion: Eight Belles. Rest in peace, sweetheart! - Judy G., Burbank, CA

"I will always remember Eight Belles' courageous race to the finish line in the Kentucky Derby just as much as I will want to forget what came after. Thank you, Eight Belles, for the gallant finish." - R. Mottin, Guelph, ON, Canada

"They say that you have to have heart. Never saw more in my life!" - C. Rich, Dallas, TX

"Eight Belles was truly a champion and a winner. May her memory live on." - D. Thomas, Rockingham, NC

"I watched you race up close at Oaklawn. I was proud of the heart and determination you showed and your love for what it is that you do. You will be missed, Eight Belles. You may go down as the greatest filly ever to run at Oaklawn Park." - W. D. White, Little Rock, AR

"Through your life and death you have touched so many and changed us." - R. Gorby, Houston, TX

"I am truly touched by the wonderful admiration showered on one of God's most magnificent creatures, Eight Belles." - M. Wilson, Canberra, Australia

"A life not lived in vain, nor for the vanity and greed of others, but a life that brought the world to its feet and may change the face of

horse-racing forever. Her legacy will always live on. You go, girl!"
- V. Hinderlider, Minden, NE

"I was rooting for this gallant filly and she did not disappoint. May this beautiful filly never be forgotten. She was meant for greater things than this world could offer." - C. L. Richardson, Ft. Worth, TX

"Because of Eight Belles, horse racing will become safer, horses will be saved, and people will someday smile again ... With greatest gratitude to her for the joy she has brought us and the joy she will continue to bring when we see the long-lasting effects she will have for all horses everywhere," - C. Bartle, Sacramento, CA

Churchill Downs agreed to ring the bells eight times at the 135th Kentucky Derby. As the bells tolled, everyone would remember the filly's magnificent run for the roses.

-13-

"Eight Belles, a gift from God above; never forgotten, always loved."
-Tribute to Eight Belles, by Stephanie L. Jones

Poems, too, were written about Eight Belles.

THE BELLS RING TRUE
by Sharon Liles Barnes

With beauty which graces only a few,
And a heart so brave, so strong and true,
A mind that knew just what to do,
The bells ring true – they ring for you.

Gray filly, fresh as morning's dew,
Waiting for her watch's cue,
A sea of track, brown not blue,
The bells ring true – they ring for you.

A long-time race, it starts anew,
Just as the colts, a blurry view,
Over the waters of track you flew,
The bells ring true — they ring for you.

As did the pace, your great heart grew,
A great gray ship, with sails wind blew,
A filly captain, all muscle and sinew,
The bells ring true — they ring for you.

Quick as a flash, the race was through,
And thus your watch was over too,
The ship had docked, and all its crew,
The bells ring true — they ring for you.

Your final watch, we never knew,
Was ending as we cheered for you,
Go down with the ship, good captains do,
The bells ring true — they ring for you.

Now comes the time to say "Adieu",
Brave, dear heart, perfect ideals beau,
Eight bells shall ring in honor of you,
In Heaven, eight more — for your life anew.

ONE SPECIAL FILLY
by Anonymous

There are some champions that gallop through our lives
And leave legacies that never die;
There are some superstars who race through the world
And who bless others' lives and shine.

There's some who win it all,
And others who take the place,
But the thing that matters most
Is that they finish the race.

There was one special filly
With a champion's heart of gold;
There was one special filly
Who left a story that needed to be told.

She didn't win all of her races,
Nor did she stay in our lives for years,
But she brought a nation to its feet
And when she left, she left a nation in tears.

Maria Michalak

There was one special filly
Who galloped into horse-racing's spotlight;
When she flew down the stretch she made us all proud,
And she finished second in the world's sight.

There was one special filly
Who faced the boys in May;
She left eighteen of them in the dust,
But she gave her life that day.

There was one special filly
Who raced with so much grace;
She gave us her all; she gave us her heart;
She finished; she finished the race.

There was one special filly;
She was one magnificent gray;
She was one awesome, brilliant girl,
And she's in our hearts to stay.

Never will she be forgotten;
Never will she be unloved,
For this precious gray Derby girl
Was sent by God above.

The King of Kings gave heaven's filly
To us on earth so we could see
A lovely piece of heaven
Gallop in the sport of kings.

Eight Belles was that little bit of heaven,
Eight Belles was a true champion and a treasure,
She was a wonderful joy and a blessing ...
And we will remember and love her forever.

A Tribute To Eight Belles, Kentucky Derby #134

THE RUN FOR ROSES
by Stephanie L. Jones

May 3, 2008
We never will forget this date.
Our hearts would fall in love so fast
With a gallant filly and her brilliant past.
Eight Belles, a beauty possessing a pure, steadfast heart,
So graceful, so valiant, in all she'd impart.
A champion whose record she would defend;
Her will and her drive sustained 'til the end.

Stride after stride, she quickened her pace,
And bravely, with valor, she finished the race.
Eighteen colts only saw her back
As she marched to the end of that royal track.

Maria Michalak

Dear, sweet Eight Belles—she gave her life that day.

In our grief, her loss is hard to understand,
But a comforting peace still blankets the land.
For we know in that instant God extended His hand,
And led our Belle into the Heavenly light.
Joyfully she dwells with Him, and she's all right.
We'll cry our tears for a little while,
But remembering her legacy will make us smile.
How blessed are we who admire and praise her,
How blessed are they privileged to love and raise her.

She brought us hope,
She brought us love,
And now she's pleasing the angels above.
A noble spirit for all to see,
She's running free,
She's running fast,
And though her earthly journey couldn't last,
What splendor she taught us,
What courage she taught us!
Eight Belles, a gift from God above.
Never forgotten, always loved.

God bless you, sweetheart. We will see you again.

-14-

"I was so proud of her ... She was a blessing in my life, and an honor to ride."-Gabriel Saez

Eight Belles was being remembered and honored everywhere. The jockeys riding at Pimlico in the 133rd Preakness Stakes wore Eight Belles patches on their boots or mud pants. The red and white patches were made by the National Thoroughbred Racing Association, with a bell, a number eight, and the word "Belles" printed on them.

Kent Desormeoux, who was in the spotlight after riding Big Brown to first place in the Kentucky Derby, said to reporters after Derby day, "I think Big Brown offered his heart; Eight Belles offered her life."

Jockey John Velasquez said, "It's something to remind everyone of a great horse. What happened [on Derby day] was a really sad thing, and we're sad. I think [wearing the stickers] is a good thing to bring awareness into our game. We'll do whatever is possible to minimize anything that happens like that."

Gabriel Saez wore the sticker, too, in the races he rode in on Preakness day, honoring the gray filly who had run so well beneath him. "She broke my heart," Saez said during an interview done shortly after Derby day. When looking back on Derby day, Saez said that all he had sensed from Eight Belles was how eager she was to run. She had never shown any signs of being injured, but had run strongly until her sudden collapse.

"I was so proud of her," Saez said, "I was so proud to be on her—second in the Kentucky Derby, 134th edition. No one can take that away from us."

Saez added, "Of course, in the Kentucky Derby, she showed that she belonged. She was a clean second. I would not have done anything differently. We had a good position and a pretty smooth trip ... She finished so well, and she finished running."

All of Eight Belles' connections—those who had been with her on Derby day and those who had been with her long before—were remembering and missing her.

Larry Jones said, "Eight Belles ran the race of her life. She went out in glory; she went out a champion to us. She was our family. We're going to miss her."

"I'll remember her as a beautiful, mild-tempered, talented filly that gave her life giving it all to be second in the Kentucky Derby," Rick Porter said.

Ron Stevens, the man who had trained Eight Belles before she went to Larry Jones, had followed Eight Belles throughout her career and watched Eight Belles race against the colts. He said, "I was so proud of her coming down the lane there [in the Kentucky Derby]. For a minute I thought she might win it, and even when she didn't, she just beat eighteen of the best three-year-old colts in the world. I couldn't believe it when they said she was down."

Charity Fillmore, who had ridden Eight Belles when Eight Belles had trained with Jane Dunn of Holly Hill Training Center, said, "I followed all of her races. It was great to see her get better and better. When she won for that first time, it was like the light turned on. When she went to the Derby, I was so proud of her."

"She'll always be close to my heart," Gabriel Saez said, "She had an incredible heart, mind, and speed. She was a blessing in my life, and an honor to ride."

Those at Fox Hill Farm thought of a way to honor Eight Belles. Wristbands were made of red silicone and embossed with Eight Belles' name. The proceeds from the wristband sales went to Midatlantic Horse Rescue, or MAHR. The idea for wristbands was inspired by the fans often on Fox Hill Farm's website and forums.

The wristbands became a huge success. The sale of over fifteen thousand wristbands helped to rescue slaughter-bound thoroughbreds.

Among the first horses rescued were a gray thoroughbred named Wheels of Stars and the bay gelding Dr. Hector, a thoroughbred who found himself one bid away from being shipped off to a Canadian slaughter facility.

Because MAHR ran out of room, they arranged with Aikindale Horse Rescue to take in a handful of horses. Some of the "wristband horses" Aikindale took in included: Choice

Request, Fast Movin Fini, Pops Dark Secret, and Socie's Girl. They also took in Skip'n True, who had made seventy starts, winning fourteen. She made over $123,923 for her connections before ending up in an auction that could have sent her to a slaughter house.

The rescues didn't stop there. Individuals were also inspired to do something in honor of Eight Belles. One of those individuals was Laura Hillenbrand, author of the book "Seabiscuit." Hillenbrand emailed a friend at the Thoroughbred Retirement Foundation, expressing her wishes to rescue a horse in Eight Belles' name.

A little earlier, at a horse auction in Vermont, a man had purchased several horses for slaughter. But he bought too many and couldn't fit the last horse into the trailer. He asked another man if he would like to buy the horse.

The other man did want to, and, with the help of Diana Pikiluski from TRF, he did. The man took the horse home and fell in love with him. Later, Pikiluski was staring at the invoice for the horse and wondering how she'd pay for him. Then Pikiluski got a call, saying Hillenbrand would like to buy a horse.

Hillenbrand became the owner of Rudster, a nine-year-old bay gelding. Rudster had made seventy-four starts in his lifetime, winning three. His final Beyer figure was a 'seven'. Shortly after receiving that figure, he was purchased for slaughter.

But because of Eight Belles, he was rescued and given a second chance at life.

Hillenbrand said, "Thank you, Eight Belles, for saving Rudster's life."

Eight Belles didn't only save lives, though. She pushed people to start thinking about how the sport of horse-racing could be made better—in her honor. Banning steroids would be the first step. Within four months after Eight Belles' tragic death, ten states had banned steroids, including the home of the run for the roses: Kentucky.

Because of Eight Belles, the 135th Kentucky Derby would be steroid-free. Twenty horses would break from the gates on the first Saturday in May, and they would finish without any help from performance-enhancing drugs, just like Eight Belles did.

Eight Belles became a catalyst for change in horse racing. Banning steroids, looking into track surfaces, making racing rules the same for each state, getting a commissioner to whom all in racing would be accountable, and banning other unnecessary drugs became her next "race."

Individuals who had never dreamed of doing anything to help make horse-racing better, suddenly felt inspired to make sure Eight Belles did not die in vain. If horse-racing could continue to become a better sport in her honor, then she would not have died in vain.

One of the groups that pushed for change in racing was the "Eight Belles Angels In Motion," better known as the EB AIMs or "the angels." They were a small group of women who met on Fox Hill Farm's website, decided that change needed to be made in the world of horse-racing, and made up their minds to do something about it.

Within a few weeks, they had created a website in honor of Eight Belles, complete with tributes to and photos of the beautiful gray filly who had inspired them so much. After some hard work and a lot of dedication, they created a petition that asked government officials to look into certain aspects of horse-racing that needed to be changed for the better.

The petition asked that a bill be passed—a bill that would improve racing greatly. They asked that the bill be called the "Eight Belles Bill." Signatures poured in from others who wanted racing to become a better sport ... all in honor of Eight Belles.

-15-

"Eight Belles, dear, rest in peace."
-Larry Jones

Picture by Candice Chavez

On September 7, 2008, Eight Belles' memorial ceremony was held at the Kentucky Derby Museum at Churchill Downs. The museum is located just a short distance from the track where Eight Belles made her final, and perhaps most glorious, performance.

Over two hundred people gathered to pay tribute to the Kentucky Derby runner-up. Some had come from as far away as New York, Colorado, and Florida to attend. Among the crowd were representatives from Three Chimneys Farm and Serengeti Stables.

While it was easy to become amazed and fascinated by the magnificence of Churchill Downs, Churchill's beauty was quickly forgotten when visitors walked into the museum and saw the large picture of Eight Belles. She was pictured with her beautiful gray head up, her ears pricked.

She was the one that everyone at the memorial ceremony had come for.

Eight Belles' leather halter, plated with her name, had been placed in a box and set near the picture. The plate on the box read: "Our Beloved Eight Belles; She Gave Her All. Kentucky Derby 2008."

The crowd gathered on the lawn at the back of the museum to watch the ceremony unfold.

Eight Belles had already been buried quietly and privately beneath a magnolia tree in the museum garden. Her grave was now covered with the many roses and other flowers so many had brought for Eight Belles and her connections.

The ceremony began with the bugler raising his trumpet and giving Eight Belles her final call to post. Just as they had on Kentucky Derby day, the notes rang out, floating on the slight breeze over Churchill Downs. Only this time, the notes weren't calling twenty horses to post, they were only calling one gray filly, the filly who had given all she had.

Lynn Ashton, executive director for the Kentucky Derby Museum, was the first to speak. Ashton first introduced the president of Churchill Downs, Steve Sexton. Sexton announced that a stakes race would be named in Eight Belles' honor on the undercard of the 2009 Kentucky Derby.

Some of the most touching moments of the ceremony came from Larry Jones, who received a heartfelt standing ovation from the crowd. Fighting back tears, Jones told the crowd some of his memories of Eight Belles. "I was the lucky one," he said, "who got to see her come into the barn as a long-legged, gangly two year old filly and was also the one who was lucky enough to see her turn into a lovely, gallant, and courageous racehorse."

Jones continued, "My memory of her on [Derby day] is that she had so much poise ... she put in such a gallant effort that day and we couldn't have been more proud of her efforts, or more devastated at what happened ... She stole a piece of my heart, and when she fell that day she ripped a big piece of my heart right out."

Jones added that Eight Belles did not die in vain. "Changes are to be made because of her. She is changing what is a good and athletic sport and is going to make it better. Eight Belles placed without the help of performance-enhancing drugs and showed us that she didn't need them—that no horse needs them."

"...I was arguing with the One who is in charge of all," Jones told the crowd, "I couldn't understand why He would take my filly, Mr. Porter's filly, and have it end this way. But it was revealed to me, thank goodness, that this was not our filly.

It was His filly a long time before we knew her, and He had a plan for her. We don't understand it right now, but we're seeing it unfold today, and we're going to see it unfold in the future."

"We will never forget that fateful day in May when our hopes and cheers turned to tears," said Rick Porter, who also received a warm, standing ovation from the crowd as he stepped up, remembering the heart-breaking collapse of his filly on May 3, 2008.

Porter said, "I hope she will be honored by being that much-needed catalyst to save our sport, for which we all have this unexplainable passion." Porter went on to say that he was surprised at how quickly change had begun, but he hoped the changes would continue, and not stop.

Porter created an Eight Belles Foundation, which will benefit horse rescues and medical research. Churchill Downs Inc. and Rick Porter each donated 25,000 dollars to the fund.

"[She's] going to make the racing game better for all of her equine peers," Larry Jones told the crowd, "They might not have to go through some of the things horses in the past have. The game is much better now than it was 50 years ago, but it's going to be better and better and better."

At the end of his eulogy, Jones turned to Eight Belles' resting place to say the words that were on everyone's hearts. "And, Eight Belles, dear, rest in peace." The heartfelt goodbye was met with a tearful standing ovation.

As the ceremony came to an end, Rick and Betsy Porter unveiled the plaque honoring their special filly.

It read: *"EIGHT BELLES*

She will live in our hearts

The magnificent steel gray

Who gave us her all

The first Saturday in May."

Picture by Kat Cerruti

And now ...

Eight Belles is still running today. Some would say that her story ended on that day in May, but it didn't. Eight Belles' story ends with incredible triumph, triumph beyond the second-place finish ... triumph that not even her breakdown could hide.

Eight Belles' amazing story ends with steroids and unnecessary drugs being banned from racing, and with horse-racing making other improvements and taking more safety precautions. Eight Belles' story ends with thoroughbreds being rescued and given a second chance at life. Her story ends with people coming together and believing that something good can come out of even the worst tragedy.

So really, her story still hasn't ended. It continues. With every improvement racing makes in her honor, and with every horse rescued in her name, Eight Belles crosses the wire in the lead, winning yet again. Her triumphs didn't end when she crossed the wire on Derby day; we are still seeing them today. Her story continues because thousands of people have her living on in their hearts. To never be forgotten is to live on, and Eight Belles is one filly that will never be forgotten.

With every improvement to the sport of kings, we can picture Eight Belles' pretty, gray head sticking out over her stall door again. We can picture her walking out to the track in the morning and galloping, ears up and brown eyes taking in everything around her.

Every year, as fillies head to post for the race named in Eight Belles' honor, we can picture Eight Belles in the post parades, going to the gates as the call to post sounded, calling her to do what she loved to do. We can picture her loading into the gates, eyes looking straight ahead to the track, eager to get out and give her best effort.

With every horse saved in her name, we can picture her bursting from the gates again, running for the pure joy of it. We can picture her leaving the others far behind, winning with ease.

In our hearts, we can picture her finishing, crossing the wire in glory. We can picture her galloping out in triumph, to the roar of thousands. We can hear the calls all over again.

"Eight Belles! Look at her go!"

"Eight Belles is fleeing the scene!"

"Eight Belles -wow!- by double digits!"

"Nobody's close to Eight Belles!"

"It's Eight Belles, a surge at the wire!"

We can picture her still running today, gray and white tail streaming out behind her, white bridle standing out on her dark gray face.

Picture by Candice Chavez

Eight Belles' Auction History

Year	Sale	Price
2006	Keeneland September Yearling Sale	$375,000

Eight Belles' Racing History

Date	Race Name	Distance	Finish	Earnings
09/16/07	Maiden @ Delaware	5.5 f	2	$8,000
10/15/07	Maiden @ Delaware	8.5 f	3	$4,400
10/30/07	Maiden @ Delaware	8 f 70 yds	1	$24,000
11/30/07	Allowance @ Fairgrounds	8 f	7	$250
12/23/07	Allowance @ Fairgrounds	8.5 f	2	$8,000
01/21/08	Allowance @ Fairgrounds	8 f 40 yd	1	$24,000
02/17/08	Martha Washington Stakes	8 f	1	$30,000
03/16/08	Honeybee Stakes (gr. 111)	8.5 f	1	$60,000
04/06/08	Fantasy Stakes (gr. 11)	8.5 f	1	$150,000
05/03/08	Kentucky Derby (gr. 1)	10 f	2	$400,000

ABOUT THE COVER DESIGNER AND PHOTOGRAPHERS

Jack McCartney: Jack McCartney, a former Standardbred racehorse trainer, has been taking pictures professionally for about fifteen years. Jack wants to thank the Porter family and Larry and Cindy Jones for allowing him to be close to Eight Belles during her career. Jack attended the Kentucky Derby to see Eight Belles run, and he designed the book cover with pictures he took of her there. Jack resides in Pennsylvania and travels to local events, racing related and otherwise, often to take pictures. To see more of Jack's pictures, please visit: www.shootinstarz.com.

Kat Cerruti: Kat met Eight Belles while the filly was at Delaware Park. She became one of Eight Belles' biggest fans, following her throughout her career, visiting her at the barn, going to Delaware Park the day Eight Belles broke her maiden, and cheering for her in the Kentucky Derby. Kat's two greatest passions are writing and photography. She wrote a story called "Eight Belles and All Is Well," which was published in a book called "Writing From The Heart," a book of compiled stories from several different authors. Kat resides on a farm in Pennsylvania with her husband and two children and draws her inspiration from the greatest words ever written, the Holy Scriptures. You can learn more about Kat by visiting: www.katcerruti.com.

Candice Chavez: A lot of the pictures throughout Eight Belles' biography are by Candice. All of the pictures Candice took of Eight Belles were taken at Keeneland, and they were all taken in one morning. The story behind the pictures is a great one.

Candice came every morning to Keeneland, but she never got to see Eight Belles. Eight Belles' workout was always over by the time Candice arrived. But one morning, there was a water main break. The break delayed all of the workouts, and Candice arrived at Keeneland just as Eight Belles was going out to the track. Candice had a choice. She could go see 2007's Horse of the Year, Curlin, take his bath, or she could go and watch Eight Belles work out. Candice chose to watch Eight Belles. It was the only time Candice ever got to take pictures of the gray filly.

"I still thank God for the water main break," Candice said, "Without it, I may never have seen her."

Candice resides in Versailles, Kentucky, and travels to the open houses and sales in her area frequently to take pictures. You can see some of Candice's pictures, along with pictures taken by many other photographers, at www.finalturngallery.com.

And one last word …

WHAT SHE TAUGHT ME
by Maria Michalak

For just minutes I watched her head to the gates;
For just minutes I watched her race;
But in those minutes I fell in love,
And cheered in excitement as she took the place.

It was only for a few minutes,
But in that time my heart she touched;
She only took on the boys for a few minutes,
But in that time, she taught me so much.

As she walked to the track,
She taught me what it means to be focused,
What it means to be ready to go,
What it means to be ready to run when gates open.

As she entered the gates,
She taught me what it means to be courageous,
What it means to step out
And walk in your purpose.

As she broke from the gates,
She taught me what it means to have grace;
Even in chaos and excitement,
Your destiny you must chase.

As she ran with the boys,
She taught me what it means to have heart,
That you must never give up,
That you must play your part.

As she neared the far turn,
She taught me what it means to be ready,
What it means to be ready to go,
So that when the time comes, you are steady.

As she flew down the stretch,
She taught me what it means to be gallant,
What it means to give your all,
What it means to be gallant.

As she crossed the wire,
She taught me what it means to be a champion,
That to give all you've got is to win,
That it doesn't matter if the numbers say you've won.

As she galloped out,
She taught me what it means to finish well;
She taught me that love never dies;
She taught me what it means to leave a story to tell.

It was only for a few minutes,
But in that short time,
She taught me that one life lived with joy
Can bless others and shine.

It was only for a few minutes,
But in that short time,
Eight Belles captured hundreds of hearts,
And left hoofprints on mine.

ABOUT THE AUTHOR

Maria resides in the foothills of North Carolina. She started creative writing in kindergarten and never stopped. She started riding at age three, got her first pony a year later, and her passion for horses grew from there. She became a fan of horse-racing in 2007, and fell in love with Eight Belles during 2008's Kentucky Derby weekend. After Eight Belles' breakdown, Maria was devastated and learned all she could about the special filly. She was amazed and honored when things fell into place for her to write Eight Belles' biography. The biography is Maria's first published work. Maria has four horses, enjoys time with family and friends (both human and four-legged), and continues to love cheering her favorite racehorses on.

LaVergne, TN USA
30 August 2009
156368LV00002B/2/P

9 781438 958095